This book belongs to

....

LADYBIRD BOOKS

UK | USA | Canada | Ireland | Australia | India | New Zealand | South Africa

Ladybird Books is part of the Penguin Random House group of companies
whose addresses can be found at global.penguinrandomhouse.com.

www.penguin.co.uk   www.puffin.co.uk   www.ladybird.co.uk

Penguin
Random House
UK

First published 2021
002

Printed in China

A CIP catalogue record for this book is available from the British Library

ISBN: 978-0-241-47630-7

All correspondence to:
Ladybird Books
Penguin Random House Children's
One Embassy Gardens,
8 Viaduct Gardens, London SW11 7BW

Peppa's Best Birthday Party

It was Mandy Mouse's birthday, and she was
having her party at Cheese World.
"What *is* Cheese World, Mandy?" asked Peppa.

"It's the most fun place *ever*!" replied Mandy.
"There's a cheese river, a cheese mountain and,
best of all, there's a cheese castle."
"Wow!" everyone gasped.

When they arrived for the party, Mummy Mouse took
Mandy and her friends to a huge cheese-shaped arch.
"Welcome to Cheese World!" announced Miss Rabbit.
"Have any of you been here before?"

"I have!" cried Mandy. "It's amazing!"
"Oh, hello, Mandy," said Miss Rabbit.
"Nice to see you back again."

Everyone followed Miss Rabbit past some cheese trees and cheese bushes. "So," said Miss Rabbit, "everything at Cheese World is about –"
"Cheese!" cheered Mandy.

"That's right," said Miss Rabbit. "And we'll start by sailing on a river of –"
"Cheese!" Mandy cheered again.

When they got to the cheese river,
two little cheese boats were waiting.
"All aboard!" called Mandy.
"And hold tight," added Miss Rabbit,
as the boats bobbed along.

"Miss Rabbit," said Peppa, "are these boats made of *real* cheese?"
"No, Peppa," replied Miss Rabbit. "They are made from pretend cheese."
"Oh," said Peppa.

"We are now entering Cheese Mountain," said Miss Rabbit, as they sailed inside a cave.

"Is it made of *real* cheese?" asked Peppa. "No," replied Miss Rabbit, "but this *is* what it would be like to sail through a cheese mountain . . ."

"Ooooh!" cried Mandy and her friends.
". . . if cheese mountains existed," finished Miss Rabbit.

After the boat ride, Mr Rabbit showed the group his Cheese Aeroplane ride. Mandy explained what to do. "If you *pull* the lever, the plane goes *up*," she said. "And if you *push* the lever, the plane goes *down!*"

Once the children were safely in their aeroplanes, Mr Rabbit started the ride. "Up, up and away!" he cried.

"This is brilliant!" said Molly Mole.
"Look! There's a sun made of
cheese!" Mandy called.
"And the clouds are cottage
cheese!" gasped Suzy Sheep.

"I can see the whole world!"
said Peppa. "It's all cheese!"

"Was that fun?" asked Mummy Mouse,
once the children finished flying.

"Yes!" everyone cheered happily.
"I told you Cheese World is the most fun
place ever!" cried Mandy.
Next, it was time to visit the Castle of Cheese.

"Hello, Mandy," said Grampy Rabbit
when they arrived at the entrance.
"Have you told your friends about
my Castle of Cheese?"
"I told them it was the best bit!"
said Mandy.

Oooh!

"It is," said Grampy Rabbit. "It's where we get to smell *real* cheese! No pretend cheese here!"

Once they were inside, Grampy Rabbit said,
"Let's start by smelling a mild cheese."

Molly and Pedro Pony both took a good sniff.
"Mmm," said Molly. "That smells nice!"
"I like it, too," said Pedro.

Grampy Rabbit sniffed the cheese, but he didn't think it had any smell at all!

"Now for something a *little bit* stronger," said Grampy Rabbit, taking the cover off a second piece of cheese. He took a big sniff. "That's more like it!" he said. "A stinky one!"

Hee!
Hee!

Pedro sniffed the cheese.
"Eurgh!" he cried. "It smells
like my daddy's socks!"

Hee!
Hee!

"And now," said Grampy Rabbit, "it's time for the strongest cheese in the **whole** world!" Grampy Rabbit carefully lifted the cover off the third cheese and took a huge sniff.

"Now, *that's* what I
call cheese!" he said.

Next, it was Mandy's turn to smell the super-strong cheese.
"Mmm . . . it's the nicest smell I've ever smelt!" she said.
"You love smelling cheese, don't you, Mandy?" said
Mummy Mouse.
"Yes!" cried Mandy. "But I love *eating* it even more!"

"Funny you should say that . . ." said Mummy Mouse.

Mummy Mouse brought out a cake covered in candles. "It's birthday-cake time!" she said. "Cheesecake!" gasped Mandy. "My favourite!" "Hooray!" everyone cheered.

"This is the best birthday ever!" cried Mandy.
"And this is the **best** birthday *party* ever!" said Peppa.